You Do!

To Dennis, Nancy, Liberty and Phoebe – K.G.
For Jessica and Emily – N.S.

YOU DO!
A RED FOX BOOK 978 1 862 30662 2
First published in Great Britain by The Bodley Head,
an imprint of Random House Children's Books
A Random House Company

The Bodley Head edition published 2003
Red Fox edition published 2004
This edition with CD published 2010

1 3 5 7 9 10 8 6 4 2

Red Fox Books are published by Random House Children's Books,
61–63 Uxbridge Road, London W5 5SA

www.rbooks.co.uk
www.kidsatrandomhouse.co.uk

Addresses for companies within The Random House Group Limited
can be found at: www.randomhouse.co.uk/offices.htm

THE RANDOM HOUSE GROUP Limited Reg. No. 954009

A CIP catalogue record for this book is available from the British Library.

Printed in China

You Do!

Kes Gray & Nick Sharratt

RED FOX

"Don't pick your nose,"
said Daisy's *mum*.
"You do," said Daisy.
"When?" said Daisy's *mum*.
"In the car on the way
to Nanny's," said Daisy.
"I wasn't picking,
I was scratching,"
explained Daisy's *mum*.

"Don't slurp your soup," said Daisy's *mum*.

"You do," said Daisy.

"When?" said Daisy's *mum*.

"On Saturday when we had chicken noodle," said Daisy.

"That's because I'd been to the dentist,"
explained Daisy's *mum*.

"Don't leave your clothes on the floor,"
said Daisy's *mum*.
"You do," said Daisy.
"When?" said Daisy's *mum*.
"Last week when you were going
to that party," said Daisy.
"I couldn't decide what to wear,"
explained Daisy's *mum*.

"Don't wear your wellies in the house," said Daisy's *mum*.

"You do," said Daisy.

"When?" said Daisy's *mum*.

"Last weekend when you came in from the garden," said Daisy.

"That's because I had to fill the watering can," explained Daisy's *mum*.

"Don't keep fidgeting," said Daisy's *mum*.

"You do," said Daisy.

"When?" said Daisy's *mum*.

"In the church at that wedding we went to," said Daisy.

"That's because the seats were too hard," explained Daisy's *mum*.

"Don't sit so close to the telly," said Daisy's *mum.*

"You do," said Daisy.

"When?" said Daisy's *mum.*

"When *you* were watching that soppy film," said Daisy. "I didn't have *my* contact lenses in," explained Daisy's *mum.*

"Don't talk with your mouth full," said Daisy's *mum*.

"You do," said Daisy.

"When?" said Daisy's *mum*.

"When your jacket potato was too hot," said Daisy.

"I wasn't talking, I was blowing,"
explained Daisy's *mum*.

"Don't lollop," said Daisy's *mum.*

"You do," said Daisy.

"When?" said Daisy's *mum.*

"Last Monday evening," said Daisy.

"I'd just done my exercises,"
explained Daisy's *mum.*

"Don't eat all the nice ones," said Daisy's *mum*.

"You do," said Daisy.

"When?" said Daisy's *mum*.

"All the time," said Daisy.

"That's because I only like the nice ones," explained Daisy's *mum*.

"Don't keep saying '**you do**',"
said Daisy's *mum*.

"You do," chuckled Daisy.

Daisy's *mum* put her hands on her hips and looked Daisy straight in the eye.
"I do not keep saying 'you do', **YOU DO!**"

"You just said it **TWICE!**" giggled Daisy.

"Right, who deserves a good tickling?" laughed Daisy's *mum*, chasing Daisy into the garden.

"I DO! I DO!"
squealed Daisy.

Really, Really
Kes Gray & Nick Sharratt

You Do!
Kes Gray & Nick Sharratt

006 and a Bit
Kes Gray & Nick Sharratt

With a free DAISY SPY KIT!

Double Trouble
Kes Gray
Nick Sharratt

Now with 8 pages of fun activities!

Yuk!
Kes Gray & Nick Sharratt

Come and play with Daisy at

Daisy Club
Kes Gray & Nick Sharratt

MEET DAISY · DAISY SHOP · FUNSTUFF · DAISY CLUB · GROWN-UPS

www.daisyclub.co.uk

Eat Your Peas
Kes Gray & Nick Sharratt

WINNER of The Children's Book Award

STORY BOOK AND CD

Tiger Ways
Kes Gray & Nick Sharratt

With free DAISY FINGER PUPPETS!

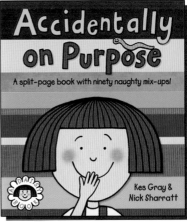

Accidentally on Purpose
A split-page book with ninety naughty mix-ups!

Kes Gray & Nick Sharratt

A Bunch of Daisies
Kes Gray
Nick Sharratt

DAISY and the TROUBLE with LIFE
by Kes Gray

With a free DAISY BOOKMARK

DAISY and the TROUBLE with ZOOS
by Kes Gray

Free Daisy BOOKMARK inside!

DAISY and the TROUBLE with GIANTS
by Kes Gray

Free Daisy BOOKMARK inside!

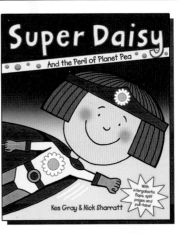

Super Daisy
And the Peril of Planet Pea

Kes Gray & Nick Sharratt

With intergalactic flaps, split pages and pull-tabs!

New longer Daisy story books!